MR. MEN
LITTLE MISS
Secret Santa

Roger Hargreaves

Original concept by
Roger Hargreaves

Written and illustrated by

Each Christmas the Mr Men and Little Miss give each other presents. Last year, to make things more fun, Little Miss Sunshine suggested a Secret Santa Christmas, where they would each secretly give a gift to one of their friends.

Everyone thought this was a terrific idea.

Everyone except for Mr Nosey.

A normal Christmas was a very testing time for
Mr Nosey.

All those wrapped presents lying under the tree were
a terrible temptation.

Mr Nosey's need to know was all-consuming.

However, once the presents were opened, then he
knew who they were from, but with Secret Santa
he would never know who his present was from.

That's too many secrets for Mr Nosey's liking!

Little Miss Sunshine wrote each person's name on a piece of paper and put them into Mr Lazy's hat, so they could each find out who they were going to be Secret Santa for.

Then they took it in turns to pick out a name.

Little Miss Neat reached into the hat and pulled out … a slice of pizza!

"I wondered where that had got to," smiled Mr Lazy.

Once they had all had a go, they carefully hid the name they had picked out.

After all, a Secret Santa had to be kept a secret!

Which was particularly necessary with Mr Nosey trying to peek over their shoulders to see who they had picked!

Some people would put a lot of effort into their presents.

Little Miss Inventor invented a pair of very clever extending stilts for Little Miss Tiny.

This year she would be able to help decorate the tree!

Mr Silly knitted a woolly ladder for Mr Small.

Not so useful for decorating the tree.

And Little Miss Helpful knitted Mr Skinny a jumper.

It will definitely keep him warm!

Most people bought their presents from the shops.

Little Miss Late was very nearly too late.

However, better late than never.

And Mr Mean was the 'never'.

Never open his piggy bank.

He was too mean to buy anything at all.

What a humbug!

I wonder who he was Secret Santa for?

We have to feel sorry for them!

Some presents were a perfect fit.

Little Miss Bossy got a megaphone.

And Mr Quiet got some earmuffs.

And some presents were not at all suitable.

Mr Slow's skateboard was too fast for him.

Mr Bounce's space hopper was too bouncy.

And Little Miss Quick's fluffy slippers were too cumbersome to get anywhere quickly!

Now, of course, the Secret Santas had to remain secret, however Little Miss Sunshine had a pretty good idea who her Secret Santa was.

Little Miss Neat could also guess her Secret Santa!

And when Mr Happy opened his present, Little Miss Shy blushed bright red, so that he instantly knew she was his Secret Santa.

At the end of a busy day of unwrapping, everyone had got their present, or so Little Miss Sunshine thought.

But Mr Nosey had missed out.

Who was his Secret Santa?

I'm sure you can guess.

Who was too mean to buy anything?

That's right, Mr Mean!

Poor Mr Nosey.

What to do?

After all that patient waiting, Mr Nosey deserved an extra special Secret Santa present.

Then Little Miss Sunshine had an idea.

She made a phone call to her friend Little Miss Christmas in the North Pole.

And everything was arranged.

Early the next day there was a knock at Mr Nosey's door.

When he opened the door, he found a huge Christmas parcel on his doorstep.

"My Secret Santa has delivered my present!" cried Mr Nosey.

He ripped the wrapping paper off in a frenzy of excitement and opened the box.

"Ho, Ho, Ho!" rumbled a jolly voice, and Father Christmas stepped out of the box!

Mr Nosey was amazed.

It was the real-life secret Santa!

Father Christmas grinned and gave Mr Nosey his very special Christmas present …

An x-ray machine!